Ghosts
Of
California's State
Highway 49

There's more than just "gold in them thar hills."

There are still folks holed up back along #49 who haven't really left us, even after they have left us.

This book is an account of some of those spooks and such who often still pester us perfectly law-abiding citizens.

© Molly Townsend 2010

All rights reserved. No part of this book may be reproduced or transmitted in any form or by any means, electronic or mechanical, including photocopying, recording, or by any informational storage or retrieval system, except by a reviewer who may quote brief passages in a review to be printed in a magazine or newspaper without permission in writing from the publisher.

Dedicated to:
…….my mom

Thanks for the bedtime stories and your never ceasing to read to me.

TABLE OF CONTENTS

STORY	PAGE
FORWORD	13
Lost Love at Melones Lake	15
Dan, Dan The Railroad Man	19
Mind Over Migration	25
Laughing Bear	29
The Ghost of the Underground	35
Just Desserts	39
The Haunting of Coarsegold Station	45
The Terror of Table Mountain	51
Scary Harry Wants A Thrill	57
Backstage Menace	61
Beware the Night	65
Judge, Jury and Executioner	71
Hot Time In The Old Town	77
Disturbance at Jackass Hill	81
A Salute To The Red, White, and Blush	87
Rip, Rush, Roar	91
Safe Behind Red	95
Sure Bet	101
The Tragic Madame of Downieville	105
Lady in Gold	111
Bootjack Bill Burns a Belfry	117
Red Dawn at Ahwahnee	123
Unlucky Spade	129
For Love of the Circus	133
Gold Bouillon	139
Author's Bio	143

FORWORD

Please take note that these stories are fictional – but reports of ghosts are so plentiful in this historical area, it is possible some of the events depicted could have taken place. Although some inspiration was drawn from researching a few distinct legends of ghosts pertaining to certain towns along California State Highway 49, this book remains a product of the creative liberty of the author. The main purpose of this book is to entertain, and I hope that my stories have accomplished just that. Thank you for reading, and enjoy!

Lost Love at Melones Lake

A beautiful stretch of road known as Highway 49 is pocketed with abundant hills and cheerful scenery, and runs across Melones Lake. To this day The lake maintains its fair share of visitors, boaters, water skiers and swimmers alike. It is a haven from the scorching rays of summer sun, and fishermen find it to be an ideal and relaxing atmosphere in which to catch their dinner. Despite the overall good nature of the place, there is what some refer to as an "underlying gloom" that can be sensed when one stares deep into the murkiest depths of the water from the bridge above. Some claim to have become suddenly and mysteriously overwhelmed with grief after gazing into the bottomless pools of dark. Some even say they have seen the hollow outline of a man's face floating beneath the surface, only briefly visible to the sharp-eyed observer. The legend begins in the early-to-mid-1860's, after Gold Rush fever began to settle down a bit in the foothills of gold country. Like most tragedies, it involves two lovers: a steam engine driver and a school mistress. Like most young lovers they were eager to begin a future together, and shortly after meeting and falling head over heels for each other began planning for a grand wedding to be held on the highest hilltop overlooking the lake. It was to take place in the peak of springtime, when the wild cherry trees were in full bloom. It was going to be a ceremony to remember, and all the townspeople spoke of nothing else for months leading up to the date.

It was just two weeks before the day of the wedding when the bride-to-be took ill, and her health began rapidly deteriorating to the astonishment of everyone who knew her. She had apparently caught some form of pneumonia and grew so weak and frail that she soon no longer had the strength to walk, and could barely raise her head from the pillow of her bed. Needless to say, the wedding was called off for the time being, in hopes that she would recover in due time. This was not the case, however. Sadly, she passed away a mere three weeks later. Everyone was in shock and grieved her passing, but none as much as her fiancée, who took it upon himself to bury her on the very hillside where they were to be married. He was so distraught at his loss that he could not bear to face a future without his love, and he took his own life by jumping to his death from the Melones Bridge.

So perhaps it is not so hard to understand why people over the years have stood by the belief that the ghost of the steam engine driver appears to those who seek it. The hollow, mournful face peers back from its watery resting place, wishing not to be disturbed, but seeking instead for a passionate and unconditional love to be acknowledged throughout the passing of time.

Dan, Dan the Railroad Man

It was the turn of the twentieth century in the quaint and peaceful town of Jamestown that the tale of Dan the Railroad Man first began.

Aside from being a prominent area of Gold Rush history, this town is also well-known for its supply of nineteenth century steam engines. The old rail yard remains a very popular tourist attraction, as the trains are still in use for visitors' enjoyment. Schools from around the area often have field trips in which the children get a chance to ride these intriguing antiques.

The story of the man simply known as Dan the Railroad Man took place in this very location. Dan was renowned in the small town for his mechanical expertise. He could fix just about anything anyone had a mind to set in front of him, from boilers and steam pumps to bicycles and pocket watches. His hands possessed a magical healing touch, some said. Dan worked on the steam engines, and was very adept at his job. His list of duties included both reparation and maintenance of the trains and the track, as well as any odd jobs and cleaning that needed to be done around the main station building. As proficient and productive as Dan was, no one ever had any complaints against him, work-related or personal. He was an all around good man with a gentle spirit and a smile for strangers. The town folks seemed to admire and adore him and the feeling was mutual.

One abnormally hot day in the middle of July work was a bit slow and laborious on the tracks due to the steadily climbing thermometer. Later on this fateful day it just so happened that one of the less commonly used steamers became derailed and crashed just a few miles short of its destination. At least a dozen passengers were reported to be dead or severely injured. Though no one shared his sentiments, Dan blamed himself for this unexpected event. No matter how his friends tried to comfort him, he maintained the belief that he could have prevented the tragedy if had proofed the track that day.

Dan's mental state gave way in the months that followed the incident, and he attempted to escape his feelings of guilt with the comfort that alcohol brought him. He quickly became an alcoholic, leading to the loss of his job as well as the respect of those who once thought so highly of him. It seemed he had lost everything he once held dear in just the blink of an eye. One rainy January morning Dan's body was discovered by a worker in the scrap metal yard of the station. He had drunk himself to death. What would have come as a complete shock to the citizens mere months before, became something more like a prediction for the way Dan's path of destruction was headed.

It's been told that strange occurrences take place in that same freight yard of Dan's early demise, tools going missing and objects being precariously rearranged overnight. One worker even reported that one of the steam engines had once been moved at least ten feet from its usual resting place. They say that it is the work of Dan's tortured spirit attempting to repair the damage he caused nearly a century earlier.

Dan, Dan, the railroad man
Fix that train as fast as you can

The whistle may blow, the boiler may fight
Just keep it up all through the night

Hammer that iron and tend that fire
A running train's what the people desire

Work your magic with those hands
To keep the pace with high demands

The tracks are calling out your name
To leave them bare would be a shame

Your achy body's growing tired
And yet your talent's not expired

The future's bright and open wide
It hangs upon what you decide

Just stay the course, you'll make it big
If from that jug, don't take a swig

Mind Over Migration

Oakhurst is the southern-most starting point of Highway 49. Today, approximately half an hour's drive to the east, is the entrance to Yosemite National Park, first discovered by white men in the mid-19th century while pursuing a group of Indians.

Soon after the discovery, there is told a story of a small group of adventurers who attempted relocation from San Francisco, via Oakhurst, to

Yosemite. In those days this was no light task, as the way would have been a geographical nightmare for horse and wagon. The mountains that envelop the path are both majestic and treacherous. As is often the case in most tales of migration, not all who began the journey ever reached their destination. This particular group set off in mid-July when most of the snow had melted from the pass, seeing how this would eliminate unnecessary risk. They anticipated perhaps weeks of hardships, but none quite as severe as what they encountered.

The group consisted of four families, totaling 13 people. They packed as lightly as possible; mainly food, fresh water, and select cooking utensils. Spirits were high and hopeful the first few of days of departure. The outlook was positive. The trail had been set by previous travelers, and little clearing of brush and overgrowth was needed. The problems first arose when one of the stronger and younger horses broke a leg and had to be put down.

This only left five horses to pull four wagons packed to the brim with supplies and people. So rotating pairs of horses was necessary to reduce the strain on any one particular animal. To the dismay of the party, this significantly slowed the pace.

Unfortunately this was not the only hindrance that occurred in the days that followed. Supposedly one of the young boys on the expedition lost his life playing near the ledge of a waterfall. This was a traumatic blow to the group whose sole purpose of migrating was to start a new life, not to have lost it in the process, especially one so young and short-lived. No one could have predicted the chaos that ensued. Numerous reparations to wagon wheels were taking place almost daily, as well as a reported grizzly attack to another horse and man that resulted in the second fatality. Nights were cold and days were tiresome. It was a constant struggle to keep moving. Disease seemed inevitable, and due to the prolonged travel time the food supply dwindled, resulting in starvation to almost all remaining. In the end only a handful of the 13 original settlers survived to reach Yosemite Valley.

The occasional backpacker hiking this route will swear on their gear that he or she has heard voices in the wind that blows over the backs of the mountain ridges and through the pines. When asked what is being said, most reply that the voices are hard to decipher, though there is definitely a melancholy undertone. A few hikers have said the words "turn back" can be distinguished when one closes the eyes and waits. A person has to wonder just what other secrets and stories are being blown about our heads, rustling in the greenery, unheard by the human ear. If only we would take the time to listen…

Laughing Bear

El Dorado County was once the proud host to a popular soda pop manufacturing business back in 1853. Today the business building is a museum, and is most noted for its two-foot-thick walls; just an interesting fact. This county is home to several Indian tribes, among them the Mi-Wok, the Maidu, and the Washoe. It just so happens that one of the tribes carries with it a legend of an ancient chief known to his people as Laughing Bear. Laughing Bear was believed to possess the power to transform objects, including human beings, into anything he desired. Laughing Bear was greatly respected, and in a sense worshipped by all for his vast wisdom of the life force and flow of nature. There was never a lingering question that went unanswered or an ounce of doubt in the tribe after an encounter with laughing Bear. Perhaps it was this security that went hand in hand with an abundance of power that gave Laughing Bear an unshakeable confidence in all his actions, whether right or wrong.

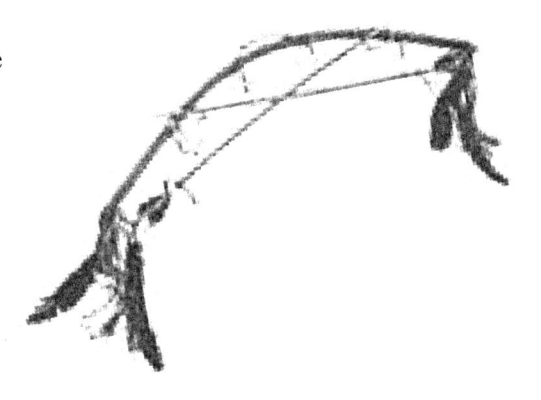

    Laughing Bear seemed to have everything he wished, and what he was lacking was soon enough eagerly given to him by any member of the tribe. There was one longing, however, that could not be satisfied with any amount of gifts or trinkets, knowledge, or servitude. This was the sacredness of love. Laughing Bear had fallen in love over the years with the wife of one of the men of his tribe. It was unfortunate, as he realized that he had no quarrel with the man called Red Hawk, aside from envy. Though he may have possessed strengths or mystical qualities equaled by none, he was after all a human being; and like every human being, human emotions were part of the package. Jealousy began to fester deep inside, taking root in Laughing Bear's innermost core. All he could think of was winning over the beautiful Padwa, wife of Red Hawk. Her smile enchanted him, and her words gave him strength. He could not rest until she was in his arms.

One bright May morning, as the men of the tribe were away on their weekly hunting excursion, Laughing Bear decided to return a bit earlier than usual in hopes of meeting with Padwa in secret. He led her away from the other women who were busy washing clothes and hides in the nearby creek.

Being extremely respectful and awed by Laughing Bear's authority, Padwa accepted his invitation to dine with him that evening in his teepee. They enjoyed each other's company immensely, as it turned out, laughing and discussing both serious and trivial matters. It seemed as though Padwa returned Laughing Bear's feelings of affection, and this merely added to his obsession with her. He decided at that time that he must act on his feelings. No matter what it took, he would not let anything separate the two of them one moment longer, for time was precious as he had always known and preached. Love would not escape him when it was so near his grasp.

Padwa and Laughing Bear spent the remaining days together, before the return of the hunting party. All was blissful and right in the world in the eyes of Laughing Bear, that is until Red Hawk reappeared. Laughing Bear put his trained and skillful mind to use developing a plan to get rid of Red Hawk once and for all. That evening he suggested to Red Hawk that the two of them make a trip into the thick of the woods in order for Laughing Bear to pass on his hunting expertise. Red Hawk agreed, and they set off at first light.

It was not until high noon, when Red Hawk was weakening with thirst and hunger that Laughing Bear used his ability and transformed his rival into a bow carved of pine. He then returned to the tribe, telling all a story of how Red Hawk was tragically killed by a wild boar. Everyone mourned the loss. Padwa remarried to Laughing Bear eventually, but she was never fully happy with him from that day on, as he could tell. Laughing Bear always carried his bow of pine with him, but it never once made a single kill for him. It was the spirit of Red Hawk making one final stand against the one who stole his love.

Perhaps it was guilt that was eating him up inside, but Laughing bear, growing weary of life as it had become, walked to the highest mountain peak one day and made the ultimate transformation, changing himself into a bear. From that day forward, it is said he roamed the forest and valleys of El Dorado County, and continues to, in search of happiness. As for the pine bow, no one is quite sure what happened to it, but it is believed to have been kept by Padwa and passed down to her son. Though ignorant of the object she possessed, she was able to keep a part of her true love with her by her side until her last days.

The Ghost of the Underground

In the town of Sonora gambling, prostitution and shootings ran rampant in the old China Town. Due to all the violence on the streets, business owners would use underground tunnels, connecting the entire downtown section, to make bank deposits. These days one would never suspect the history of this sleepy town's wild past. During the 20th century there was talk of installing utility wires underground, but the tunnels made this impossible. The Red Church, built in the 1800's, and other local buildings have been sinking a little each year, probably due to these tunnels.

There is a legend of what some refer to as the "tunnel bandit" who practically lived underground, relying on such cautious business owners to use these passages in order to steal their wealth before they could make it to the safety of the bank. Jacky D. was one such bandit, who was only known as the Ghost of the Underground. It took several years for the townspeople to realize it had been just one man making the attacks. Store owners began to travel in pairs through these tunnels after the ghost had struck nearly three dozen times. By the time the pattern was established, business owners decided they should retaliate. It had become a complete toss-up as to which route was safer: above amidst the town violence, or below with the Ghost of the Tunnels.

A small band of business owners decided one day to trap this ghost like one would trap a mouse. Three of the men used a bag full of stones as a decoy, making their way as usual through the main tunnel en route to the bank, while three more men armed with guns waited at a cross-section to a second tunnel half-way to the bank. Though this was a good plan in theory, it failed. The men in waiting never met the ghost, or even heard the cries from the three with the decoy, which had been taken from them nonetheless, rocks and all. The ghost had done it once again, without so much as a whisper, vanishing without a trace. This left the men to believe there were more tunnels that had yet to be discovered, for how else could one explain the last charade? No one, however, had the will to search any further for the mystery hide-out or the mysterious Ghost Bandit.

So the legend lived on a few more years, for as long as the ghost felt the urge to take. He may have moved on to some other town eventually, wishing to face the light of day. But for all we know, those tunnels may very well be his grave.

Just Desserts

The mischievous Tommy Tucket grew up in Lotus, El Dorado County, not far from the 16-to-1 mine. He was born into a wealthy family, and received just about anything his pudgy, greedy fingers reached for. At the age of twelve, Tommy had become quite a nuisance to the townspeople, for everyone knew what to expect when running into this whirlwind of trouble. Tommy had sticky fingers when it came to passing through candy shops and toy stores. It wasn't as though shop owners didn't notice, but mainly they let it slide, wishing to avoid a confrontation with Tommy's parents. It was common knowledge that wealth bred power in the work force, and no one wished

to lose their means of support due to one crummy kid's kleptomania. So they all kept their mouths shut and went about their business.

    Unfortunately the disrespect didn't stop there. Tommy used foul language to his peers, elders, and even complete strangers he passed on the street. He once strapped some firecrackers to a stray kitten he found in an alley, and made two school girls watch as he lit them, laughing the whole way through. It was clear to all that Tommy was a bad seed, rotten through and through. If only someone had the nerve to stand up to it all. It's what everyone secretly prayed for at night, but wouldn't dare mention in the light of day to the random bystander.

It just so happened that in this very town there was a person so full of nerve that it was bound to seep out his crevices one way or another. They called him Bloody Bill Williams. With such a name one can only imagine what the man was capable of. Bill wore a belt adorned with human teeth, said to be from men he had killed in bar fights, or simply for looking at him in the wrong manner. At a startling 6 foot 6 inches tall and weighing 285 pounds, it was hard to imagine how anyone would be senseless enough to pick a bone with this beast of a man, but there are always exceptions. One thing was certain: everyone respected him out of fear, and maintained their distance if they knew what was good for them.

It was Tommy's misfortune to choose Bloody Bill to aggravate on a day when the man had lost nearly $250 on a lousy poker hand, but that was just the way of things. As he was lumbering out of the local saloon, mud pies and pebbles bombarded Bloody Bill. He looked up to see his assailant was none other than little Tommy, grinning his twisted foxy grin, hands clasping his most likely stolen, prized slingshot. Bill was not one to stand for such foolishness, and quicker than a snake bites its prey, grabbed the youngster by the shoulders, his veins visibly throbbing with fury. He took him out back behind a tool shed, and without so much as a word, did away with the rascal and hid his body somewhere in the 16-to-1 mine shaft.

It can't be said that the town was broken up about Tommy's disappearance in the weeks to follow, but somehow they all suspected it was Bloody Bill's doing, and this made them equally as uneasy. No one valued his life so little as to go running to the law, and the way they viewed it, it was a favor that had been granted them. No more terrorizing of the locals, or endless shenanigans when least expected; or so they thought. It wasn't until a short while after the ordeal that people started noticing things going missing in their shops, sometimes even after hours, and overnight. They were horrified to discover writing inside the windows, as if smeared with dirty fingers, and sometimes even on the walls dirty words were scribbled with a red crayon. It all made sense to the citizens' dismay, once they began to hear laughter and actually see Tommy's face appear briefly in windows of local establishments. It seemed that trouble was there to stay, and there was just no escaping it. That may have had something to do with almost half the townspeople of Lotus pulling up stake and seeking refuge elsewhere within the year…just a guess.

Such a handful Tommy was,
Playing tricks just because.

A rotten apple to the core,
Sparking rage like none before.

Those dirty games he used to play
Could drive a man insane they'd say.

All good things would come undone
When adding to the young boy's fun.

He'd laugh and sneer at people's pain,
yet all their scolding was in vain.

But now young Tommy's in the ground,
It didn't pay to kid around.

The Haunting of Coarsegold Station

Coarsegold fire station, west of Highway 49 just outside of Oakhurst, holds within its walls quite an intriguing mystery. Firefighters for many generations have witnessed strange occurrences inside the station, such as lights going out downstairs, numerous tools and equipment such as masks, boots, and hose going missing or turning up in odd places.

Of greatest interest, the image of a young man age 18-20 appears to many a worker near the fruit trees planted out back. The young man always wears a brown leather cowboy hat with a peacock feather for protection sewn into the lining.

These occurrences have happened so often for so many years, that one day one of the firefighters decided to do a bit of research in his spare time. He soon discovered that back in 1858, what was now the fire station used to be a ranch. Not only this, but he also found out that a young man was hung out back in a barn for being a horse thief. Where the barn used to lay was now overgrown with many cherry trees and plants, and where the mysterious young man was always seen. This seemed to explain the ghost as well as the odd electrical failure and the missing equipment. Upon further extensive investigation, they were able to uncover more of the history behind the young lad who was hung.

The horse thief, called Bobby James, lived with his sick mother and three younger sisters. The family was poor, and every day was a struggle just to survive. Bobby worked as a ranch hand, and the two older sisters did their part by sewing and selling what they could, though all together the income was barely sufficient to feed five mouths, and keep a roof over their heads in the cold, snowy winters of Coarsegold. Eating soon became a luxury, rather than the norm. It was hard times for Bobby's clan. Providing for the family took a toll on poor Bobby, as he was working ten- to twelve-hour days, doing all he could to keep from falling asleep in the saddle while on the job.

One day Bobby snapped under the pressure, and gave in to the temptation of taking a pair of beautiful young Arabian stallions he had been eyeing for a while. They were exquisite in every way, with their refined bone structure, high tail carriage, and feisty spirit. His idea was to sell them for a pretty penny, for he knew of several ranchers out of the area who would be willing to pay what he asked. Unfortunately for Bobby, one of the workers happened to catch him on his way out, and immediately reported him to the boss. The boss, a stern, broad shouldered man with an unforgiving nature, gave the orders to string the young thief up in the rafters of the barn as a lesson to all who might have been considering cheating him. He then burned Bobby's prized hat and kept his belongings so that his family wouldn't have a thing to remember him by. Apparently a human life had been the cost of the almost-loss of two horses in the eyes of a heartless, hollow man.

To this day young Bobby appears from moments in time, ever searching for a way back to his beloved family, perhaps to explain to them the reason behind his actions.

He did what he could out of love for them, wishing nothing more than to take care of them and make them happy. He will never stop trying. So if you by chance visit Coarsegold station in days to come, and Bobby happens to appear to you, please send a smile his way for me. He deserves it.

Are you sleeping Bobby?
Your working day's not done
You'd better get those barrels stacked
And beat the setting sun

Are you sleeping Bobby?
Don't you rest your head
It's up to you to earn enough
To keep your family fed

Are you sleeping Bobby?
Ignore your bleeding hands
Your duties must be carried out
Before all other plans

Are you sleeping Bobby?
Don't let time be delayed
Keep busy with hard labor
If you are wishing to be paid

The Terror Of Table Mountain

Table Mountain lies on the outskirts of Jamestown and can be seen to both the left and right when driving west on Highway 49. In the springtime it is quite majestic, inlayed with lava rocks practically buried in wild flowers of all colors of the rainbow. It has always been a beloved area for nature-lovers to trek about on lazy days.

An old hermit by the name of George H. Jimmson used to reside in his comfortable little shack of a house on top of Table Mountain. He grew and supplied his own food so he would really never have the need to go to town. To be frank, people frightened him. He didn't know how to interact socially, and this made even the slightest human contact overwhelming. Kids would always pick fun at poor George for being such a recluse. He had, to nobody's knowledge, ever been married, or ever had any living siblings, or any sort of family for that matter. It was a sad situation indeed, for no one should ever have to go through life so alone. Yet the children who vandalized his house and dug holes in his yard didn't seem to understand this, unfortunately. The meanest trick they ever played was writing a love letter to George and signing it with the name of Isabelle Franklin, the prettiest, most prestigious lady in town.

George, being naïve from all his years of seclusion from everyday life, believed this letter to be real. It was his curiosity and fascination with his pretend admirer that caused him to venture into town one day. He wandered cautiously into a feed store to ask for the address of Isabelle, which he eventually got after much hassle. He knocked on her door, holding a dozen red roses in his hand. She answered, and was appalled when he confronted her about the love note that she never wrote to him. She was very harsh with her words, and basically told him he stood absolutely no chance with her, or with any other woman in town.

Had she spared him his dignity, he may have recovered from the embarrassment he felt. But the way things played out, it was clear to George that it was a mistake going there, as well as a mistake in thinking that people were kind and loving.

From that day on George remained locked away in his shack, and took to terrorizing anyone who dared trespass on his property. The youngsters who used to mess with him soon got a taste of their own medicine. The old hermit would let his hounds loose, or even shoot at their heels, forcing them to run in horror.

He found that hurting others gave him a small bit of pleasure and satisfaction with his disappointment of a life. Soon nobody wandered near George's residence out of fear for their safety. George remained on top of the mountain until the day he died, never again to journey back into the town that wouldn't accept him to begin with. It is such a misfortunate that one person's actions could have such a negative effect on his perception of all people, though this is generally how such reservations about life develop.

After George's death, his body wasn't discovered until many weeks later, when a government official finally came by to collect taxes. The shack was later burned down, but many swear on their own grave that George's angry spirit roams Table Mountain, scaring grazing cattle, or killing off wild flowers, causing as much chaos as he can muster up.

There was an old hermit
Who lived on a hill
Those who dared trespass
He'd threaten to kill

The anger inside him
Burned ever-strong
He never considered
His actions were wrong

Those boys they would taunt him
From noon until night
Of course the old hermit
Would put up a fight

He'd pick up his rifle
And fire some rounds
To scare those cruel youngsters
From off of his grounds

And yet they persisted
To torment his life
Perhaps things would be different
If he'd had a wife

Scary Harry Wants A Thrill

    Columbia State Historic Park hosts many exciting and fun activities to date, specific to the Gold Rush era: panning for gold, stage coach rides, and many old-time stores, restaurants, ice cream parlors, and candy shops where the workers dress in 19th century fashion. Demonstrations are also occasionally put on for the public. There is also the Fallon House Theatre that puts on numerous plays of all genres, which is a very important piece of Columbia's history. A pleasant afternoon can be spent roaming the streets of the old town.

In the days of bonnets and coattails lived a stage coach driver named Harry, last name unknown.

Harry was a middle-aged, light-hearted man who very much enjoyed his job, and very much enjoyed riding his coach at a maximum speed. He thrived on adventure, and took any opportunity that presented itself to test boundaries of safety and normalcy. The man despised routine. This presented a problem for his chosen profession, as most passengers felt uneasy under Harry's care. Regardless, they were unable to pick and choose. Harry was one of the few drivers in the town of Columbia, fortunately for him.

En route to a neighboring town, Harry was one day ambushed by a gang of highway robbers. Caught completely unaware, his two passengers were robbed blind by the bandits. In the blink of an eye the thieves were gone, but not without Harry soon tailing close behind, in a gallant attempt to regain what was stolen from his defenseless passengers. It was his chance to shine.

Urging his horses ever faster, he was determined to catch up, and was soon within arm's reach of his rivals. It was the chase of a lifetime, such as in today's movies. At this point the reader should know that Harry was alone in the coach, as his two passengers had previously un-boarded out of fear. Harry was hot in pursuit of the getaway gang, but as fate would have it, a snake in the grass spooked one of his horses, causing them both to run the coach over the edge of a forty foot precipice. Harry did not survive, but had an unmistakable grin spread across his face through to the last moment of his life.

Occasionally a man driving a stagecoach wildly through the clusters of boulders throughout Columbia State Park can be glimpsed. It is believed to be Harry, getting his kicks and thrills even in the after-life. He will not give up the chase.

Riding like a cyclone
Through an easy going town
Harry had a one track mind
No one could keep him down

Well he'd feel kind of lonely
And he'd feel like a bore
Until he took his reins in hand
And then he'd start to soar

The wind spat in his face
The wheels spun like a blur
Old Harry treated every day
As if it were a race

And such a sight it was to see
That man fly round about
Without a worry in the world
So light, so bold, so free

Since Harry left this curious earth
It's plain as night and day
A fire burned in his blood
From the very second of his birth

Backstage Menace

The Opera Hall, located in Sonora, is renowned for its many musical programs and concerts put on for the public's enjoyment. It is a rather high-class affair, and attendance is never lacking under any circumstance. What the audience observes onstage seems to always go according to plan, from piano concertos to traditional Irish step dancing, always charming, professional, and serene. With absolutely no visible flaws, the audience would be shocked to learn what quirky disturbances lurk behind the curtain. There have been rumors of disturbance backstage dating back to the 1900's, blamed on ghosts of performers past.

Reportedly, it all began when the one forbidden name of theatre was spoken out loud on the premises. Performers of all sorts can be extremely superstitious about this occurrence, for whenever the name "Macbeth" has been said aloud inside or around the performing hall something terrible happens. The first performer to utter the word during a rehearsal was run over by a horse and carriage immediately after exiting the building.

From that point on every time the name was spoken in the building, someone ended up either dead or seriously injured from props falling or ladders giving way beneath someone's feet. There was even a death due to a fire caused by spilled kerosene on the curtain and a careless toss of a cigarette. Perhaps the most disturbing incident linked with the misuse of the forbidden name was when a musical director of much prestige hung himself from the rafters backstage the following day. This came as a total surprise to all who knew him personally. Many believed that there was no reason for his suicide, and concluded the only explanation that could have pushed him to it was supernatural in nature.

So over time it has become a rather serious issue to hold to the tradition and refrain from speaking "the name" within the theatre world. There is even an procedure that has been developed to counter the curse, which includes turning around counter-clockwise several times and spitting over the left shoulder, in an attempt to prevent disaster at all costs. Performers do not take kindly to practical jokers wishing to get their kicks by testing the superstition. If you have this in mind, you'd be wise to hold your tongue. Just a friendly word of advice.

Beware The Night

Not much exciting ever happened in Murphys, California, aside from the occasional festival celebrating the excellence of local food and wine. That's not meant to subtly imply that these festivals are dull or overrated; only to re-iterate the fact that the town has not seen much in the realm of extraordinary over the years. This was the case, at least, until the legend of Biff Potter, self-proclaimed vampire.

There's so much that could be said about Biff Potter, like the fact that he never went out in the daylight, causing his pasty skin to become almost luminous in the soft glow of candlelight; or the way he avoided human contact as much as possible, so as not to be tempted to take a gnaw on the necks of the good townspeople. Actually, the majority of the townspeople weren't quite sure if they believed in the existence of such creatures, so they simply wrote Biff off as a delusional, schizophrenic lunatic. The evidence suggested otherwise. Besides his pale complexion and obvious hermit-like tendency, there was the fact that livestock was disappearing at the rate of about one cow or goat each week.

Now, people either blamed this on hungry coyotes, a likely possibility; or in a less conventional theory, Biff was to blame. The reasoning figured. Biff believed himself to be a creature of the night, one of the living dead, a vampire. Everyone in touch with folklore and mythology has heard that vampires must drink blood for sustenance. That is common knowledge. Therefore it was entirely possible, according to the ranchers and others aware of this strange occurrence, that Biff was acting on his delusion and feeding off these animals for nourishment.

Yikes! Regardless if you believed Biff to be a vampire or not, popular opinion soon shifted under the unified belief that Biff was the cause of the missing livestock. This was due to the influence of Stanley Stevens, a sort of local hero. One drunken evening he got to discussing the issue with his congregation of bar fellows and soon concluded this was the case. Any thought or opinion exhaled its way into absolute truth when coming from Stanley's lips. Naturally the townspeople agreed with his accusation. It was after all somewhat logical, albeit disturbing, that this would be something Biff would do, or at least be interested in trying.

Stanley Stevens was short-tempered, impatient, and extremely violent when it came to defending his position, yet the people loved him. This respect Stanley got wasn't deserved or even earned, for he certainly had none for other members of the community. Instead, this respect was simply flung at him, mostly out of fear and ill-conceived admiration. The worst part of it was that Stanley believed himself to be worthy of this respect, and more. There seems to be at least one of these chauvinistic narcissists in every small town.

On the previously mentioned evening, after a ritual six or so mugs of tap brew, Stanley and his followers decided it was time to take matters into their own hands. What Stanley said went, so naturally there was no opposition or even murmured question of doubt when he proposed a good old-fashioned tar and feathering of the supposed vampire. So away they marched, pitchforks in hand, to give Biff a piece of their unified mind.

Upon reaching Biff's dominion, a desolate hillside manor nested comfortably beneath boughs of ivy, the people began to shout insults in order to entice their opponent to appear. Biff was many things, but he was no coward. He stepped onto his balcony to face the incensed crowd. Before he had the chance to inquire as to what the problem was, a shot rang out, resulting in Biff Potter toppling over the balcony's edge. It turns out Stanley

had concealed a pistol in his coat pocket, and in his drunken state, had not hesitated to put it to use. Biff Potter was surely dead. But when the mob climbed the forested hill to recover the body, they found it was gone. No one could believe their eyes! They had all witnessed the shooting, the startled look in Biff's eyes. They had seen him grab his chest, undoubtedly a fatal shot, yet there was no body to show for it. The whole situation was just absurd.

No one reported the whole truth of what had happened, merely that Biff had disappeared into the night. But those who were not present that night did not find anything peculiar about it. Biff, whatever he may have been, was in a league of his own. Life continued on for the people of Murphys as it always did. It seemed the Biff/Stanley ordeal was enough excitement to last the town for the next several years, allowing them to slip comfortably back into their peaceful, glacial pace of things.

Over the next twelve decades, through the withering and ever-changing hands of time, Biff's presence has methodically been noted on the night of the full moon when he chooses to appear. Perhaps the reason for this being that the full moon indicates the end of a cycle, or the death of the old in preparation for the new. Very symbolic indeed to someone like Biff Potter, but then again he was a strange one…

Judge, Jury, and Executioner

Travelers of Highway 49 should be sure to pencil in a stop at Mariposa's County Courthouse, the oldest California courthouse, and impressively still in operation since its humble beginnings in 1854.

Home to Yosemite National Park, this county is over-flowing with natural beauty, majestic mountains, and rolling grasslands.

It is quite a sight to behold. During the 1850's, the Honorable Justice Henry P. Hendrik lived a comfortable life full of leisure and limitless respect from the multitude of Mariposa citizens. They treated him as some sort of Deity, practically bowing at his feet for the noble cause his esteemed position served. During the course of his career, he had put away countless murderers, bandits, and unstable loopy-loos unfit for society. The people were grateful for this, and felt an unwavering safety under his Honor's watchful eye. Perhaps one talent that Justice Hendrik possessed that the town did not fully recognize was his power of words. He used his words as an artist uses his brush, a bold instrument, and a one-way ticket to attaining the desired reaction of the public.

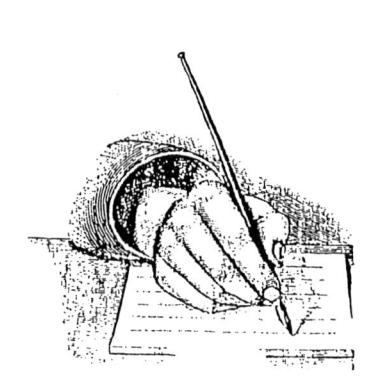

One could say that through his careful emphasis of word selection and placement, he had the power to manipulate his jury into siding with his personal agenda…as he did one day.

You may wonder what the seed of Justice Hendrik's corruption was that led to the breaking of a sacred oath to serve justice free from bias and personal gain. It turns out that, like many situational dramas of life, it had to do with jealousy.

Mr. Jebb Holland and Ms. Caroline Johnston were absolutely infatuated with each other. Not a day passed when the two weren't seen together laughing, or when they weren't embracing each other as they meandered through sun-kissed meadows or pine-laden trails on their peaceful way to nowhere in particular.

Ms. Caroline was a portrait of beauty, amplified by raven-black locks, ruby lips, and an electric green gaze. It was no surprise that the hearts of many men were held captive under her spell, including Justice Hendrik.

No one was aware of his affection for Ms. Caroline, of course. This would be improper, seeing as how she and Jebb were engaged to be married within the next two months, not to mention that he was nearly twice her age! The Justice never made any obvious attempt to pursue the young lady's affection, other than the occasional good-natured joke about the bizarre state of politics, or the recommendation of good local eateries. All in all, no one so much as suspected his secret desire, as it was so deeply buried in the core of his being. Jealousy and obsession, however, were beginning to poison his every thought, and he was soon enough consumed by the deluded fantasy that he and Ms. Caroline could, and should, be together.

It happened that Justice Hendrik caught a lucky break one day when Jebb was brought before him in his court of law. Jebb was accused of murdering a local man. The victim was Marshal Kyle, killed outside a local saloon with one shot to the back of the head. Folks had every reason to believe that Jebb was guilty, as he was seen hovering over the body, drunk out of his mind, and with his recently-fired gun on the ground. The evidence pointed to Jebb's guilt, except for the fact that he had no visible reason to kill the man and no witnesses to testify that he did.

Though Jebb pleaded his innocence before the Judge and Jury, Justice Hendrik jumped on the chance to convict his rival of the crime. He skillfully wove together the fabrics of prejudice and hate, and gently let them flow into the minds of each member of the jury. Before the day was over, Jebb Holland stood convicted of murder in the first degree and was sentenced by Justice Hendrik to be hanged the following day.

After Jebb's execution, the Justice gathered the courage to make his intentions known to the grieving Ms. Caroline, for which he was adamantly rejected. The poor woman could hardly look at her lover's executioner without the purest loathing, and rightly so. Who could blame her?

It was at this time that Jebb's brother let it be known that he suspected foul play and corruption of the law on the part of the Judge. He made his belief known to as many people as possible, and idea soon gained validity in the eyes of most. This belief was further strengthened when another man of the town admitted to the killing one evening under the influence of strong whiskey. He actually bragged about it to a couple of cowboys, for which he was immediately apprehended. The whole situation was an outrage.

As for the professional and private life of Justice Hendrik, he was frequently haunted by apparitions of Jebb in his courtroom from that day forward. Though he never admitted this to a single soul, it was plain to see that these disturbances steadily drove him to madness. He ended up fleeing the town before a year was over, never to be heard from again.

Through the telling of this tragic tale, the faith in the power of authority was weakened to some extent. On the other hand, it seemed to the people of Mariposa that justice had truly won out in the end.

Hot Time In The Old Town

Coulterville, located at the junction of Highway 49 and 132, was originally given the name Banderita by the Mexican miners in 1850. Banderita means "little flag." The name was given after founder George W. Coulter's small American flag was seen hanging outside his tent. The name eventually evolved into Coulterville in 1872.

As is the case with many gold rush towns, fires were one of the biggest threats, and Coulterville was plagued with multiple fires throughout the nineteenth century. Even so, many historic buildings have been preserved. Oddly enough, there were three fires that decimated the town, occurring exactly twenty years apart in 1859, 1879, and 1899, always in July!

This phenomenon, if you could call it that, is largely believed to be the work of a restless spirit, a miner who lost his life in the fire of 1859.

The Coulter Hotel was re-built mostly from stone after the 1859 fire destroyed the original wood structure. The theory here is that a twenty-year-old man, an Irish immigrant worker, was trapped inside the hotel on the third story during the outbreak of the fire. He never made it out alive.

It's possible the dates of the two sequential fires are twenty years apart for the significance of the victim's age at the time of his death. The rebuilt Coulter Hotel, with the first two floors made of stone, was burned down yet again in the fire of 1899. No one can speculate the reason for the end of the forty-year-reign of the ghost of the Coulter Hotel. Perhaps he is merely taking a break. Or perhaps three times is indeed a charm. Only time will tell.

Disturbance at Jackass Hill

A replica of Mark Twain's cabin can be found on Jackass Hill Road between Sonora and Angels Camp. It was here that Mark Twain spent three months one summer visiting the Gillis brothers, mining for gold and relaxing in local establishments and saloons, while gathering ideas for stories such as his infamous, "The Celebrated Jumping Frog of Calaveras County."

In the 1800's, Jackass Hill was a stopping point for pack trains headed from Stockton to Sonora. The name Jackass Hill was bestowed due to the braying of the packs of donkeys that could be heard for miles around. The cause of the braying, however, is up for interpretation, though popular belief blames the disruption on restless spirits stirring up tension.

* * *

The ghost of Jennifer Jamison often startled the good people of Angels Camp, and yet it seemed they had so grown strangely accustomed to hearing multiple accounts of her ghoulish behavior, the fear that would normally have ensued was eased. The type of spirit who would rattle chains and upset furniture or damage property simply because she could, Jennifer seemed to genuinely enjoy causing an uproar. It seems that her mischievous nature in life followed her into death as well, for better or worse.

In life Jennifer Jamison had been a vibrant, voracious individual. Always ready to grab the world by its four corners and shape it into whatever she desired, she was not one to let good things slip from her grasp. She believed strongly in creating her own luck, as well as her own happiness through the decisions she made.

It just so happened that what Jennifer desired ever since she was a little girl was to become a blacksmith. This was generally unheard of for a woman of the 1800's, as it was considered a man's trade, dealing in dangerous and strenuous use of equipment. But Jennifer did not let this stand in her way. She bore the criticism of her neighbors and friends and practiced for hours on end every day forging hundreds of shores shoes, wagon axles, tools, knives, axes, and even eventually fashioning guns.

Jennifer didn't mind being covered in soot and ash and reeking of smoke, because she loved her work and took pride in the objects she created. She became very skilled with an anvil, and fire soon became her best friend and closest companion. It didn't matter what people thought, or what snide remarks they made behind her back. She was living her dream and the satisfaction of this accomplishment outweighed any need for approval.

Jennifer quickly earned a reputation in the town for being exceedingly good at her job, and she gained plenty of business to the dismay of local competitors. Her success was a breeding ground for jealousy among male blacksmiths who disapproved of her choice in occupation, causing them to feel almost inadequate at the thought of being bested at their prize jobs by a woman. It was one of these bitter competitors who was responsible for the death of Jennifer Jamison.

One day as Jennifer was finishing taking inventory of her tools, a rival blacksmith snuck into her station and opened the bellows so much that the fire jumped wildly out of control. Roaring flames licked the wooden beams of the ceiling. Jennifer was over-whelmed with despair upon the discovery and attempted to recover her most valuable tools, but the smoke and heat was too much to bear. She soon collapsed from exhaustion, never to wake up.

Her death became known to the town, but sadly, was written off as nothing more than a tragic accident. Perhaps this oversight is what stirred Jennifer's spirit to her rambunctious actions. She is suspected to have been the one taunting the packs of donkeys responsible for the noise heard every so often - and for which Jackass Hill was named - by pulling the ears of the donkeys, spooking them with her eerie screeching, clanging noisily, rustling the trees.

When the owner of one pack came to see what was causing the uproar in one instance, he found nothing out of the ordinary; nothing except for a single black anvil lying in the grass.

A Salute To The Red, White And Blush

Plymouth is located at the north end of Amador County on Highway 49, in the heart of Gold Country. Noted for its family-operated wineries and Zinfandel wines, the cup never runs dry in this region.

Paul Tucket, proud citizen of Plymouth in the 1880's, enjoyed a good glass of wine. To be more precise, the man enjoyed several glasses of wine on any given day. No matter the occasion, even when there was absolutely no occasion whatsoever, he spent hours sipping away, training his taste buds to fully appreciate the complexity of dry, sweet, red, blush or white wines. Paul could find his way between the cellar and a corkscrew in record time. He considered himself a connoisseur of fine wine, and took pride in his vast knowledge of the fermenting process and its effect. Paul very well should have been skilled in such techniques, as it was his job as a wine taster to provide an accurate description and critical review of the various wines that Plymouth produced.

This talent Paul developed soon enough became his purpose in life. Friends grew concerned with his obsession with wine. In a few months time he was consuming close to ten glasses on a daily basis. All feared it would surely be the death of him.

It was not, however, the wine that killed Paul one late November evening as he sipped a sweet Port, seated comfortably before a crackling fire. No, it was instead the strychnine that the wine was laced with that did the job.

Poison seemed such an odd way for Paul to go, but the way in which it was administered made complete sense to everyone. The only positive light that people seemed to make of the situation was that at least he died doing what he loved best: drinking. The question of who slipped the poison in the bottle still remained a mystery, though it was more than likely a rival connoisseur who felt severely threatened by Paul's success. No one knows for sure.

What people did know, however, was that after Paul's death things around the wineries just didn't seem to go right. Grapes aged prematurely on the vines. Bottles curiously uncorked themselves overnight. Any and everything that could go wrong at the local wineries did for a period of seven unlucky years before regaining financial stability. The citizens of Plymouth have the wine-soaked spirit of Mr. Tucket to thank for that losing streak.

Rip, Rush, Roar

Built over the Stanislaus River in Stanislaus County in 1864, Knights Ferry's covered bridge holds the title of being the longest covered bridge in California. Stretching a lengthy 355 feet, wooden beams crossed in every which way create ample support to bear the weight of hundreds of pedestrians at a time, though it was closed off to vehicles over two decades ago due to the heavy vibrations weakening the beams.

The bridge is now operated by the United States Army Corps of Engineers.

The original bridge of 1842 was actually demolished when a second bridge upstream crashed through the covered bridge, a result of raging floodwaters brought about by over-abundant rainfall. In fact, the whole town of Knights Ferry, including the mill, lay in ruin after the incident.

Prior to this unexpected summersault of nature, an even greater tragedy occurred on the river in this location. One of the mill worker's sons was drowned beneath the strong current of the river's misleading, calm exterior. Sadly, the people of the town really had no previous warning as to the extremity of the river's pull. The boy's body was never recovered, but it is rumored his spirit has never quite left the river.

In the springtime each year following the boy's drowning, poppies explode in one obvious cluster beneath the bridge in the very spot where his life was lost. Visitors during this period have remarked on the heart-warming oddity that met their eyes.

    The entrance to the bridge is occasionally decked with vibrant petals of bright orange. Even after being blown away the petals always seem to repopulate atop the aging floorboards, a seasonal reminder of the sanctity of life. No matter the length of time we possess it, may its radiant colors ride boldly on the wind for all eyes to see and all minds to ponder.

Safe Behind Red

Perhaps passersby have often wondered what the motivation was behind the stylistic choice of the Red Brick Schoolhouse in Altaville. The color red has always held significance in this world for an assortment of reasons.

In nature the color is more than not a sign of caution to all animals, warning them to keep their distance out of fear for their life; a reminder that even the smallest of creatures can possess the most potent venom. In society we have come to recognize red as a call to yield, as seen in stop signs and red lights for the direction of traffic. It is the color of blood, the color of hearts, and the color of life as some would argue.

There was once a traveling salesman known only by the name Mac who happened to pass through Altaville in its primeval stages. Mac sold just about everything: Antique dishes, tobacco, pipes, soaps, mittens, socks, whistles, harmonicas, jewelry, pocket-knives, pocket watches, figurines, paintings, and even bubblegum. If you could picture it, chances are Mac had it for sale.

This salesman made pretty good business wherever he went, but especially in Altaville, where not many shops had yet been established. Mac quickly made friends with the townspeople over a period of days. People were eager to buy his knick knacks, and equally as eager to hear his stories.

Words flowed eloquently from his mouth, as if he were weaving a fine tapestry fit for a Persian princess.

These stories had no boundaries and no discernable purpose other than to entertain. People enjoyed Mac's tales of mountaineers coming face to face with grizzly bears, living to tell the tale; or how he himself once survived three days without food in an Alaskan snow cave before being rescued by passing sled dogs. No one could be sure if the stories were completely factual, but they took his word for it.

So on his last day in town before journeying onwards, Mac told perhaps the most intriguing tale he'd ever told. It was about a close friend of his who was captured by what appeared to be a band of pirates, while vacationing off the coast of the Spanish Main in the 1830's. His friend was enslaved to work the deck of the ship for several weeks, being fed small rations of bread and limes in return for his cooperation.

These pirates had what appeared to be no heavy artillery aboard the ship, though the pistols they wore strapped menacingly to their belts were enough to keep their prisoner in line. Mac's friend had given up all hope of being rescued after one month of imprisonment, but then the tides of change brought luck to the unhappy man when a passing naval ship opened fire on the unidentified vessel.

The pirates remained aboard to the very end until sunk to the depths of the ocean bottom, while their only prisoner jumped ship to embrace his rescuers, who were mildly shocked at the spectacle before their eyes.

Ever since his capture, Mac's friend swore on his mother's grave that the ghosts of the Spanish pirates followed him over the years. No matter the country he ran to, or the people he surrounded himself with, those eyes would always be on him, their smiles and whispers in the night robbing him of countless hours of sleep and sanity. Nothing worked to prevent this disturbance until his friend moved to the country in a new house built of red bricks.

Sleeping in this red brick house provided Mac's friend relief from his nighttime visitors. It was a sanctuary set apart from the restless spirits of the night, throughout which he was never once awakened by tortured laughter, or by shots of gunfire during which he would find them there staring. He revealed to Mac that though uncertain as to why, he attributed his newfound peace to the red bricks. His eventual conclusion was that they provided a shelter from evil, warding off spirits who meant harm.

So upon hearing the testimony of Mac's friend, it was agreed that no harm could be done in constructing the children's schoolhouse in Altaville from red bricks, just in case.

Sure Bet

Mokelumne Hill, bypassed by Highway 49, was prime Mother Lode gold country soil in its time, with discoveries of gold being made in amazing quantity. The popular entertainment of this era was the bull and bear fights put on by the town for the miners' amusement. This was also a means to gamble away, or if luck would have it, win, money and nuggets by placing bets on the outcome of the fight.

In these fights a grizzly bear would be put into a ring with one or two bulls, depending on size and estimated strength. The stakes could be high for the occasion, with blood pulsing and hopes on the rise that sound judgment was used in the selection of the victor. More often than not, it was a game of chance with no sure hand one way or the other as to which animal would be left standing.

Often these games would escalate to steamy brawls ending in broken bones, black eyes, busted teeth, and even on the rare occasion death would result. This sadly proved the hold that money and the prospect of wealth had over people, and the extreme lengths they would go to achieve it.

A sullen-faced giant of a man called Jim Bradley once placed a bet on Red Fury, the 680 pound grizzly standing nearly six feet tall with claws sharp as butcher knives. Just staring at this bear from ten feet away was enough to make a grown man wet himself. In all his confidence, Jim bet his prized gold nugget he'd found the week earlier, which held an estimated value of about $2,200. He, like many others, felt that it was a sure win.

Even paired against two raging bulls practically spouting steam from the nostrils, all odds were in favor of Red Fury. The majority of miners bet large sums on the brute of a grizzly, but when one of the bulls struck a sudden blow from behind, a riot broke out in the crowd.

The onset of that surprise attack led to a downward spiral from which Red Fury was unable to recover.

Blow after blow the bulls rushed the unsuspecting grizzly until he lay in a crumpled mass upon the bare earth, barely capable of lifting his enormous head. No one could have predicted that turn of events.

Jim, amongst plenty of other furious gamblers, did not take his loss with dignity. He began smashing unfinished bottles of whiskey he'd grabbed from the hands of bystanders, cursing at the top of his lungs in a drunken rage. The men he'd offended were equally as drunk and upset over the outcome of the fight, and before you could count to three, half the crowd was throwing punches and flailing knives at each other. Gunshots rang out, and by the end of the chaos, seven bodies lay cold in the grass.

These seven miners who lost their lives that day allegedly have not strayed from their place of rest atop Mokelumne Hill. On the contrary, they seem to appear as a group in the very spot where they took their last breaths, sprawled face down in the dirt, arms linked in peaceful protest.

It is at the moment when a person questions the validity of what their eyes have just been witness to that the startling image vanishes before the brain has time to comprehend it. The wind blows, and birds carve patterns in the mellow blue sky as if nothing has, nor ever will, change in years to come. The earth holds fast the secrets that will seldom be told.

The Tragic Madame of Downieville

The gold rush town of Downieville, located at the fork of the Yuba River, was a hotbed for the practice of fluming in 1851, though the outcome was not entirely profitable, seeing as how the cost of these flumes outweighed the gold retrieved from the river. The modern Downieville excites tourists yearning for a scenic mountain getaway, and offers the opportunity of fishing or panning for remnants of gold in the streams.

This town was once the site where one of a scant number of women were hanged during the gold rush period, a darker page of California history.

Perhaps Madame Marina deserved her sentence, or perhaps it was due to irrefutable provocation that drove her to bash the head of Mr. Kerry in full view of several men outside the Crazy Horse saloon. None of these men could fathom that Madame Marina, such an elegant, fine-turned, dignified woman would commit such an act of atrocity.

The question on every upstanding citizen's mind over the next several hours was "why?" What had driven such an esteemed lady to murder? Many questioned whether she was momentarily possessed by a demon. The fact of the matter was that Madame Marina had killed Mr. Kerry clear as day. No one could argue this.

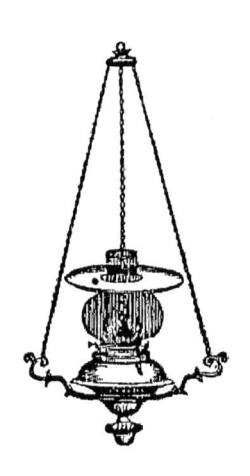

As she sat calmly in her cell awaiting her due trial, onlookers would try to sneak a peek through the barred window at the doomed lady in waiting. Some men who had not preoccupied their minds lamenting the possible loss of such an alluring beauty even placed wagers on the severity of her sentence. Most figured the judge and jury would go easy on her, being an attractive, upper-class female. There were, after all, very few documented cases of a woman being executed.

It turned out it was the worst case scenario for Madame Marina. Her upbringing and her beauty could not save her in the end. She was sentenced to be hung by the neck until dead the following day. Such a pity it had to come to this.

Miners came from surrounding towns out of curiosity from what they'd heard. Women strayed from their houses, hoping for little ones not to trail behind. All of Downieville and beyond gathered on the bridge above the gushing waters of the Yuba River that fateful afternoon.

Mist rose and spat on the faces of the crowd, in contrast to the quiet and unsettling tranquility of

Madame Marina. Throughout the entire walk to the noose her expression did not change. She did not utter a single word or bat an eyelid up to the release of the hastily constructed planks from beneath her feet. Everyone hesitated to breathe too loudly, and only the boisterous roar of the rapids below was audible.

The question of why Mr. Kerry was struck down by Madame Marina remained a mystery. People did not mourn the loss of him so much as they did the woman who, in all 28 years of her life, had more than gained the respect and admiration of locals with one small wave of her hand and blush of the cheek. Still, no definitive conclusion could be made in conjunction with her actions.

In years to come Madame Marina left her mark upon Downieville, haunting the bridge above the majestic Yuba River. The wood would creak and moan menacingly beneath those who dared trod it; a caution of its dark history. Over-sized branches would fall into the pathway of walkers, resulting in more than a few injuries, not to mention shocking them half to death.

Every so often there would be reports of men jumping to their deaths from the bridge, or in some cases "falling" to their watery grave. Some believe these deaths stemmed from the coaxing and convincing whispers of the tragic, yet illustrious Madame of Downieville.

Lady in Gold

Gold Lake, located north in Sierra County, is part of the Lakes Basin Recreation Area, comprised of several small snow melt lakes that are surrounded by the towering Sierra Buttes. The final stretch of historic Highway 49 comes to a halt nearby. Fishing, camping, and a varied selection of hiking trails are sure to satisfy the adventure-seeker's craving. In winter, Gold Lake Road is closed, though the area's frozen beauty is a paradise for those who enjoy skiing and snowmobiling.

Few people, especially those who are surrounded daily by such a landscape would care to delve into the realms of the paranormal; however, beneath such beauty lurks the legend of The Lady in Gold.

She wears a calf-length evening gown of gold silk with a prominent bow adorning her dropped waistline, undeniably flapper-style fashion of the 20's. Her short brown hair is topped with a cloche hat that brings out her visibly darkened and seductive eyes. She appears to boaters and fishermen alike on the water's edge.

Her tragic tale is left to the creativity of the imagination, for she does not speak. Men fall madly in love with her after the first, and likely only look they will get of her in one sitting. They yearn for just another glance, and spend their days circling every square inch of water for that look.

There is no pattern to her coming and going, merely when it suits her. Some days she is seen sitting on the short, beneath the lengthy branches of the pines. Some days she wades knee-deep into the water and gazes to the mountains.

Some fishermen claim they've gotten, however brief, a close enough look at her to read the sadness in her eyes. They say it's a gently heartbreaking image, and that a person can tell with one look everything she once aspired to be. Perhaps there's a story behind that despondent stare. There most always is.

A handful of these men swear they recognize her from old photographs in newspapers as a nightclub singer of the 20's who went by the name of Hattie Lombard. At the height of her career Ms. Lombard went missing, never to be seen again. Popular theory is that she was murdered by a jealous fiancée who suspected her of having an affair with the owner of the nightclub. If in fact this was the case, no evidence of foul play was found.

Whatever trials this young woman went through in life, it seems as if she has claimed the lake as her refuge from haunting memories of the past. As a siren of still waters she remains, unable to let go of all she had, capturing the eyes of those lucky enough to see her, the cat's meow dressed in shimmering gold.

In those eyes lie mysteries of old
Consuming countless hearts
A vision clad in gold

How they yearn to earn her smile
She merely tilts her head
And stares at them a while

Her secrets cast a shadow in the day
By night an eerie glimmer
That never fades away

Her milky skin the moon illuminates,
And still her past unknown
Stays locked behind closed gates

She wades into the watery abyss
Waves her graceful arm
Then gently blows a kiss

Nature swoons each time that she appears
The rain is stopped
Revealing stifled tears

A fragrance rare as gold lingers in the air
Sweet pine and spice
Makes all the world aware

She wraps her soul in memories secured
And utters not a sound
Her thoughts remain unheard

Bootjack Bill Burns a Belfry

Bootjack is located in Mariposa County. "Bootjack Bill" happened to be the least popular member of the Bootjack community in the year 1867 on account of his blunder of the burning down of the town's belfry.

No one ever held a grudge against the man, for he was a hard worker with sound morals who was constantly prepared to help out his neighbor, yet after the fiasco there was not a soul who didn't loathe the very air he breathed. Much pride and joy had been bestowed in that bell tower, the product of 75 men's hard labor over a four-year construction period. To have it destroyed in such a manner was the ultimate slap in the face.

Bootjack Bill, as he became known after being chased from the town by an angry mob with pitchforks in hand, never intended for things to accelerate into chaos as they did. In fact, he never meant to cause harm to anyone or anything, but as the saying goes, "the road to hell is paved with good intentions."

Bill loved his town and its inhabitants. He loved the way in which strangers, though the only strangers were passing travelers on account of the relatively low population, were helped and pampered without expecting the favor to be returned. Everyone knew each other, and looked out for each other. It was basically as near to a utopian society as one could get; that is, until Bill jolted the natural order of

Bootjack and tainted the unsuspecting, open minds of its friendly dwellers.

At the time, nothing seemed like a better form of flattery to show his appreciation to the town than by decorating the prized belfry. It was to be Bill's personal contribution. He put his plan into action one moonlit, starry night.

Under the cover of darkness, Bill gathered together two dozen pink roses, and a fistful of chrysanthemums. At the last moment he decided that a lit torch in the center of the open tower would be a marvelous touch to his décor. So he wrapped a gasoline-soaked rag around a four foot torch and pocketed some matches, making his way to the top of the belfry.

After a grueling climb of ninety steps, the plan was put into effect. The colorful flowers strewn on the sills of the open frame really did their job of brightening things up, but it was poor timing when the caretaker hollered from below at Bill as he was lighting his torch. The man believed Bill to be up to no good upon seeing fire in the belfry. The shout startled poor Bill, causing him to drop the torch. It fell to the floor below where a conglomerate of woodchips and newspaper accelerated the flames to spread to the beams, eventually setting the entire structure ablaze.

Bill managed to escape death by climbing down the outside of the wooden tower, only to face the scorn of the group that had quickly assembled in the night. They stood in awe as flames lit up the sky, and their blood boiled along with the heat that the most dangerous of the four elements emitted.

Forgiveness was erased from the thoughts of the crowd in the minutes that followed. Bill tried to explain himself, saying the whole thing was an accident, but the people would not listen. The crowd grew, and attitudes became all the more soured.

The most important fact in their mind's eye was that the belfry was no more, and that Bill was to blame for reasons they did not care to uncover.

All patience was replaced with hostility. It soon became clear to Bill that mercy and compassion were far distant from the realms of the situation. So as the angry faces approached him, he began to run as fast as his legs could carry him. He ran through fields, forests and beyond the county line until he could no longer recognize his exact location. It was only at this point that he felt safe enough to retreat into what began a new life for him, separate from those he used to know and care for.

It was rumored that Bill moved up and down the coast of California in the remaining years of his life, never able to fully settle in any one location for fear of being run out; an unfortunate side effect of his poor outlook on life.

Many years after his death, Bootjack Bill is still blamed whenever anything bad happens in the town, regardless of the severity. His ghost is believed to be a prominent force of mayhem and misdeeds, trying to settle the score for an unhappy past.

Bootjack had a belfry
So very, very tall
The citizens of Bootjack
Had to watch that belfry fall

    And who's to blame
    For such a mess?
    A clumsy man
    We must confess

Yes, Bootjack Bill has done the wrong
Now in this town he can't belong

Red Dawn At Ahwahnee

Historic Ahwahnee was established when settlers of the gold rush years fully intended to strike it rich with the discovery of the precious metal. They discovered something unexpected, but perhaps equally as valuable in the long run; rich, fertile soil in which they grew fruits and vegetables to sell to local mining camps. This proved to be quite profitable. President Theodore Roosevelt once stopped in Ahwahnee to have a bit of lunch while on is way to Yosemite, which naturally made headline news, and was a pleasant surprise for the blossoming town.

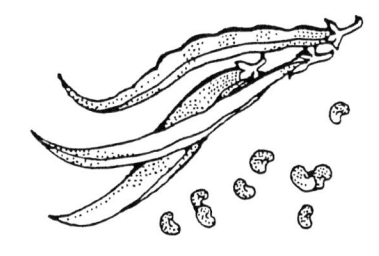

Interestingly enough, a tuberculosis sanitarium was built in Ahwahnee at the turn of the century, with the hope that the fresh and pure air would benefit sufferers of the disease.

This train of thought was good in theory, but it was thwarted by one of the sanitarium's very own on the medical staff. Campers near the area tell the story of the psychotic Doctor Norman Wellsley, a sadist who preyed on his defenseless patients like a lion would a lamb.

It's been told that the unsettling images of past patients roam the forest near local campsites. Their hollow faces remain expressionless as they seek in vain solace for their senseless murders. They are garbed in grey hospital gowns, tattered and stained. Sometimes they cry out in the dead of night, but their lungs fail to deliver much more than an exaggerated whisper. Barefoot, they tread the muddy, rocky terrain, though it could hardly impose any damage in their ghostly state. Irreversible damage has already been done that even the passing of centuries could not wash away.

What drove the successful Dr. Wellsley to commit such atrocious acts one might ask? It may have been due to a bad childhood, or to an improper balance of chemicals in his brain, but whatever the case, the fact of the matter is that he *did* commit them, and reveled in the pleasure he attained from doing so.

Dr. Wellsley was a full-blown psychopath whose entire purpose of being in the two years he worked for the sanitarium was to end the lives of as many patients as he possibly could. He carried this out by taking one patient at a time, when he fancied the time was right, out into the woods. He'd tell the patient it was for the purpose of getting fresh air and alone time, which would be good for the mind. After gaining the patient's trust, and ensuring seclusion, the doctor would strike. He usually strangled his victims, who were in no position to fight back due to their weakened state brought about by the disease. He then did his best at hiding the bodies in the areas where the violence occurred.

Finally, after two years of slaughter, the doctor confessed to his crimes, boasting of them. His confession was not out of a sense of remorse for his actions, but rather alleviation from boredom with the routine. Workers of the sanitarium were of course appalled and shocked to hear this. The doctor was immediately taken to prison and executed a short time later. It was estimated that at least a dozen patients fell victim to Dr. Wellsley in those two years. Twelve bodies were found, but the doctor would never reveal a number. There may have been more for all they knew.

If anything can be learned from this tragedy, it is the sacredness of a life. The lives of at least a dozen innocent people were cut short by one man in whom they put their trust and hope.

They were not dealt a fair hand, but such is life. All the more reason to live with the greatest vigor and ferocity one can muster.

Campers who've seen the apparitions swear that they are attracted to light, especially the blaze of cozy camp fires. Maybe they are hoping to connect with the warmth of kind-hearted individuals such as they themselves were in life; one last encounter with a gentle soul before moving on to whatever lies ahead.

Dr. Wellsley was not well
Though no one else on earth could tell

He sipped his coffee, read the news
Sometimes he'd even shine his shoes

But something deep within his mind
Made the doctor quite unkind

The confidence of all he met
He gained without a drop of sweat

Yet Dr. Wellsley played a game
Sick as his twisted lack of shame

When watching patients slowly die
He wouldn't even bat an eye

But on his face you'd find a smile
A triumph that would last a while

Then soon enough that smile would fade
So he'd repeat the hand he'd played

For two whole years he kept this up
Until his ego tipped his cup

For those the doctor blithely killed
Know that justice was fulfilled

Unlucky Spade

In January of 1848, gold was discovered in Coloma by James W. Marshall while building a saw mill for John Sutter. Word of the discovery, despite attempts to keep it secret, spread like wildfire, and people began flooding into the area from all four corners of the globe. This began what became known as the California Gold Rush.

Coloma, located in the foothills of Highway 49 and the south fork of the American River, is today dedicated to being a State Park. Every January, in honor of the discovery, people dawn period clothing and life of the 1840's is reenacted.

Mickey Donovain was a miner who never left his house without his black felt hat; an eagle's feather and an ace of spades were stuck in it. It was his good luck charm. It was with this very hat that he won a high stakes poker game, claiming $2,500.00 a few years prior, and he had never been without it since.

It was early one excruciatingly hot summer afternoon in 1849 when Mickey's relentless hours of panning for gold had finally paid off. He dragged in a whopper of a nugget, about three inches in diameter. His excitement could not be contained. Mickey began to shout in jubilation.

His cries attracted one nearby local man, who, believing no one to be watching, struck Mickey in the back of the head with a shovel after glimpsing his triumph. The blow killed Mickey. Overcome by greed, the man pocketed the nugget and took off to the nearest assayor's office in a hurry.

In the process of getting to the assayor's office, the thief's reckless behavior got the better of him. He pushed his horse to run at a breakneck speed through a very rocky terrain. The hoof of his horse got caught up in a large pothole, resulting in a broken leg, which required the horse to be put down. The horseless man then had to walk the remaining five miles by foot.

In the final stretch of his vigorous trek, as fate would have it, the worn out villain was bitten in the calf by a rattlesnake. He never saw it coming. Oddly enough, the man decided to stick to his original plan of heading to the assayor's office to collect the worth of the nugget before finding a doctor. Perhaps he could then afford to pay for the medical bill, if he managed to live through it.

Getting nearer to death with each passing minute that he waited for the nugget to be appraised, the man sat in agony. Five minutes passed before the assayor returned to announce to the pale-faced, half-conscious man that his prized nugget for which all had been sacrificed, including a human life, was nothing short of fool's gold. The man, engulfed in self-pity, reached down to comfort his swollen leg. It was then that he noticed the playing card that had fallen from Mickey's hat into his boot…the lucky ace of spaces.

> *It all was lost*
> *On that same day*
> *When fate won out*
> *And had her way*
> *The evil done*
> *Was turned around*
> *In one brief moment*
> *Luck was drowned*
> *To no avail*
> *Your hand was played*
> *It rested all*
> *Upon that spade*

For Love of the Circus

Nevada City is considered by some to be the best preserved as far as Gold Rush towns are concerned. The town is decorated with Victorian-style houses, booming pines, and historical buildings including 18 registered landmarks. The population today is close to 2,500, about a quarter of what it reached at the peak of gold fever.

Just before the turn of the century there lived a young girl in Nevada City by the name of Tina Tinsel who absolutely adored the circus. She loved the exotic dress of performers, the smell of freshly popped corn that wafted through the air, the colorful painted faces, and risky tricks of fierce animals. Most of all Tina loved the tight rope act. It was by far her favorite part of the show. She admired the brave woman who took her life in her own hands, and held it up at a height of 30 feet for all to see.

Every year when the circus would come through town, Tina was sure to be found in the first row, eyes fixed on the tight rope walker, scarcely drawing breath for fear of disturbing her hero's concentration. She couldn't help but imagine what fun it must be to scare so many people at once, all the while feeling confident in your steps.

The idea to become a professional tight rope walker slowly grew on her over the next several years, and by the time Tina was 18, she had begun her training. Tina started off walking at the friendly height of four feet. If she fell, which she often did, it would be of no great concern. After a couple hundred tries, Tina felt compelled to move the height up by another three feet. Eventually this became a comfort zone for Tina's ever-growing skill as well.

After a little over a year of practice at 10 feet, Tina felt it was time to reveal her talent to the town. With the help of a friend, she stretched a 20-foot rope between the chimneys of two equally level rooftops. She announced her endeavor to all who would hear it. She, "Tina Tinsel the Tight Rope Walker," would perform the feat of a lifetime from a height of 25 feet. This news attracted half the town to come and see the girl with such gusto. People murmured to one another their doubts, believing Tina to be half-witted or insane for feeling compelled to showboat such a dangerous stunt. Tina could not be talked down. She stood tall on the ledge of her starting position, looking proud and at ease in her pink tutu and umbrella. Her confidence didn't sway as she took her first step onto the rope, and then the next foot. The crowd below gasped. She was actually doing it, living her dream. Everyone seemed a bit shocked at how capable she appeared to be. A mixture of awe and panic emanated from below.

It was a little past the half-way point when things took a turn for the worse. A sudden gust of wind hit poor Tina from the side, causing her to lose balance and topple over. Twenty-five feet was a fall too great to survive.

Ever since the disaster, people take notice of the dancing figure on the rooftops whenever the circus appears. She twirls about, dressed as on the day she fell. She wants nothing more than to fulfill her life's ambition by finishing the breath-taking stunt she began so many years ago.

Don't look down
Into the sea
Of all your fears below.
Just keep your gaze
Set on the stars
Which light the dreams you know.
So take a step
Of confidence
And may you hold your ground
Then take a breath,
And let it in
With all the peace you've found.

Gold Bullion

Mount Bullion derived its name supposedly from Senator Thomas Hart Benton, father-in-law of John C. Fremont, after being nicknamed "Old Bullion" for his devotion to hard currency. Mount Bullion is located seven miles south of Bear Valley, northwest of Mariposa along historic Highway 49, and today hosts a very minimal population with few remnants of the mining era, such as the Trabucco store, the Princeton Saloon, the old Mount Bullion Schoolhouse, and the deserted Princeton Mine.

Benton, or "Old Bullion," served on the senate as a senator and representative from Missouri in the years 1821-1851. The senator was an advocate for western expansion, and pushed for hard money, or currency backed by gold. He even proposed a law that only hard currency was to be used in payment for federal land, though this proposal was shot down. This was largely done for the purpose of encouraging settlement of the west in the pursuit of territorial expansion of the United States.

The old Princeton Mine near Mount Bullion was originally owned by Fremont, and produced in its time around $4.5 million worth of ore. It has been deserted since 1927, but still it is believed that a yet undiscovered fortune lurks in its depths.

A handful of Mount Bullion residents have taken note of strange goings-on. At night a pale yellow light from a lantern can be seen from the entry to the mine, swinging back and forth. It's almost as if the keeper of this flame is signaling to someone to join him in a search for prosperity.

A ghost, people claim, is responsible for the midnight light show. He is diligent in his crusade for Manifest destiny, believing there to be an abundance of gold pocketed among the rocks; enough wealth to prosper the nation that Senator Benton was so fond of. It appears this search will never cease, though by chance a lucky soul may someday uncover what his restless spirit has yet to do. Then maybe he will finally be ready to set down his lantern and rest.

Old Bullion, don't stop searching
Keep searching for that gold
No matter what the others say
You'll never be too old
A prize that lies below the earth
Enough to spur a nation's birth
It rests on you, dear senator
Old Bullion, don't stop searching

Author's Bio

I was born in California and grew up in Jamestown from the age of four. Highway 49 runs through the north side of this little town, which has a population of a little over 900. The first fifteen years of my education were completed while living in Jamestown. I am currently studying at Chico State University after recently completing a year of study in Germany. Journalism is one of my areas of study. Writing has always been a passion of mine, and something I hope to continue to pursue throughout the years.

I feel very fortunate to have been raised in an area filled with such immense cultural and geographical history.

GHOSTS OF INTERSTATE 90 Chicago to Boston   by D. Latham

GHOSTS of the Whitewater Valley by Chuck Grimes

GHOSTS of Interstate 74   by B. Carlson

GHOSTS of the Ohio Lakeshore Counties   by Karen Waltemire

GHOSTS of Interstate 65   by Joanna Foreman

GHOSTS of Interstate 25 by Bruce Carlson

GHOSTS of the Smoky Mountains by Larry Hillhouse

GHOSTS of the Illinois Canal System by David Youngquist

GHOSTS of the Niagara River   by Bruce Carlson

Ghosts of Little Bavaria   by Kishe Wallace

Shown above (at 85% of actual size) are the spines of other Quixote Press books of ghost stories. These are available at the retailer from whom this book was procured, or from our office at 1-800-571-2665 cost is $9.95 + $3.50 S/H.

- **GHOSTS of Lookout Mountain** by Larry Hillhouse
- *GHOSTS of Interstate 77* by Bruce Carlson
- **GHOSTS of Interstate 94** by B. Carlson
- **GHOSTS of MICHIGAN'S U. P.** by Chris Shanley-Dillman
- GHOSTS of the FOX RIVER VALLEY by D. Latham
- *GHOSTS ALONG I-35* by B. Carlson **by Roger H. Meyer**
- **Ghostly Tales of Lake Huron**
- Ghost Stories by Kids, for Kids by some really great fifth graders
- Ghosts of Door County Wisconsin by Geri Rider
- *Ghosts of the Ozarks* B Carlson
- **Ghosts of US - 63** by Bruce Carlson
- *Ghostly Tales of Lake Erie* by Jo Lela Pope Kimber

GHOSTS OF DALLAS COUNTY	by Lori Pielak
Ghosts of US - 66 from Chicgo to Oklahoma	By McCarty & Wilson
Ghosts of the Appalachian Trail	by Dr. Tirstan Perry
Ghosts of I-70	by B. Carlson
Ghosts of the Thousand Islands	by Larry Hillhouse
Ghosts of US - 23 in Michigan	by B. Carlson
Ghosts of Lake Superior	by Enid Cleaves
GHOSTS OF THE IOWA GREAT LAKES	by Bruce Carlson
Ghosts of the Amana Colonies	by Lori Erickson
Ghosts of Lee County, Iowa	by Bruce Carlson
The Best of the Mississippi River Ghosts	by Bruce Carlson
Ghosts of Polk County Iowa	by Tom Welch

Ghosts of Interstate 75	by Bruce Carlson
Ghosts of Lake Michigan	by Ophelia Julien
Ghosts of I-10	by C. J. Mouser
GHOSTS OF INTERSTATE 55	by Bruce Carlson
Ghosts of US - 13, Wisconsin Dells to Superior	by Bruce Carlson
Ghosts of I-80	David youngquist
Ghosts of Interstate 95	by Bruce Carlson
Ghosts of US 550	by Richard DeVore
Ghosts of Erie Canal	by Tony Gerst
Ghosts of the Ohio River	by Bruce Carlson
Ghosts of Warren County	by Various Writers
Ghosts of I-71 Louisville, KY to Cleveland, OH	by Bruce Carlson

Ghosts of Ohio's Lake Erie shores & Islands Vacationland by B. Carlson
Ghosts of Des Moines County   by Bruce Carlson
Ghosts of the Wabash River   by Bruce Carlson
Ghosts of Michigan's US 127   by Bruce Carlson
GHOSTS OF I-79   ***BY BRUCE CARLSON***
Ghosts of US-66 from Ft. Smith to Flagstaff   by Connie Wilson
Ghosts of US 6 in Pennslyvania   by Bruce Carlson
Ghosts of the Missouri River   by Marcia Schwartz
Ghosts of the Tennessee River in Tennessee   by Bruce Carlson
Ghosts of the Tennessee River in Alabama
Ghosts of Michigan's US 12 by R. Rademacher & B. Carlson
Ghosts of the Upper Savannah River from Augusta to Lake Hartwell   by Bruce Carlson

Mysteries of the Lake of the Ozarks Hean & Sugar Hardin								
GHOSTS OF CALIFORNIA'S STATE HIGHWAY 49 **BY MOLLY TOWNSEND**								
Ghosts of La Salle County by Joan Kalbacken								
Ghosts of Illinois River by Sylvia Shults								
Ghosts of lincoln Highway in ohio By Bruce Carlson								
Ghosts of the Susquehanna river By Bruce Carlson								
Ghostly Tales of Route 66: AZ to CA by Connie Corcoran Wilson								
Ghosts of the Natchez Trace by Larry Hillhouse								

To Order Copies

Please send me _____ copies of *Ghosts of California's State Highway #49* at $9.95 each plus $3.50 for the first one and $1.50 for each additional copy for S/H. (Make checks payable to **QUIXOTE PRESS**.)

Name _____

Street _____

City _____ State _____ Zip _____

QUIXOTE PRESS
3544 Blakslee Street
Wever, IA 52658
1-800-571-2665

To Order Copies

Please send me _____ copies of *Ghosts of California's State Highway #49* at $9.95 each plus $3.50 for the first one and $1.50 for each additional copy for S/H. (Make checks payable to **QUIXOTE PRESS**.)

Name _____

Street _____

City _____ State _____ Zip _____

QUIXOTE PRESS
3544 Blakslee Street
Wever, IA 52658
1-800-571-2665